The Book Swap

Liz Hedgecock

WHITE
RHINO
BOOKS

To the volunteers: the people who step up and get things done

GNU Terry Pratchett

1

'*Becca.*'

Jolted out of her thoughts, Becca jerked upright. Everyone in the room was looking at her.

'Sorry,' she said, 'I was miles away.'

'We saw,' said the chair of the Parent-Teacher Association, a gilet-wearing, tousle-haired, immaculately manicured woman called Saffron. 'Would you like a recap?'

'Please,' said Becca. There was a huff from halfway down the meeting-room table where Mrs Hanratty, the teacher member of the PTA, was sitting.

'So,' said Saffron, 'we were just discussing the book swap.'

'The book swap?' Becca already regretted her decision to join the PTA. *It'll be a way to meet people and make friends*, she had thought, after a week of standing on her own in the playground at drop-off and pick-up, watching the other parents chat and giggle. *A good way to get back into doing things again. Low pressure.*

When the letter about admission to primary school had arrived, Becca realised with a shock that the decision would affect not just the next seven years of Ellie's life, but hers too. *Can I stand another seven years of this?* she thought, as she stirred a mug of packet soup after she had finally got Ellie to sleep. *No money, no social life, nothing but Ellie. And the local schools aren't up to much.* So she had done some research, moved to a small flat in leafy Meadley, and got Ellie into the excellent primary school.

And now here she was, facing the members of the PTA. With everyone around a large table, the meeting reminded her of *The Apprentice*, except the participants seemed far more capable and fearsome. So far, items on the agenda had included pulling strings to replace the school iPads with the latest versions, bidding for funding for solar panels, and organising an exchange visit to Nice so that year six could practise their French. Becca, who had expected a bake sale or maybe a school disco, slid down in her seat as figures flew about the room, along with words like logistics, leverage, and interoperability. Was that even a word?

'Yes, Becca, the book swap,' said Saffron, with a hint of weariness. 'Frankly, I'm as unimpressed as you sound, but in the absence of anyone else, here we are.'

'I'm afraid I don't—'

'You're new to Meadley, aren't you?' said Heather. If Saffron was Level Five scary, Heather was a three. Her gilet was fluffier, her nails less pointed, and Becca had actually seen her smile. 'The book swap is a former phone box on Beech Lane, not far from the school.'

'Oh,' said Becca. 'I come the other way.'

'I daresay you do,' said Heather. 'Now, the book swap is nothing to do with the school, but the thing is that old Mrs Val, who usually looks after it, is having a hip replaced and will be out of action for some time. As the school is nearby, the parish council asked us to take ownership of the book swap for a while. Literacy, and all that.' She waved a dismissive hand.

'I still don't see why the older children couldn't take it on,' said Saffron.

'SATs prep,' snapped Mrs Hanratty. 'Plus health and safety. You don't know where those books have been. With some of them, you wouldn't want to.'

'There's nothing to it,' said Heather. 'Checking it maybe once a week, removing any books which aren't fit to be there, tidying the shelves…' She eyed Becca speculatively. 'You said when you introduced yourself that you're not working right now.'

'I will be looking for a job once Ellie has settled

3

in,' said Becca. 'So I definitely couldn't commit to anything long-term.'

'Oh, it wouldn't be long-term,' said Heather. 'Just until Mrs Val is back on her feet. I'm sure she'll be raring to go before we know it. A contact from the council told me the Best Kept Middle-Sized Village inspectors will be paying Meadley a visit fairly soon, so we really must look our best.' She smiled at Becca, who was suddenly very aware of her faded jeans and the frayed hem of her top. She glanced at her nails and winced. She'd fallen into the habit of chewing them again.

'If someone else wants to do it, I won't stand in their way,' said Becca, in a last-ditch attempt to swerve her duty.

'It's not that I don't want to do it,' said Heather, 'but I'm already leading on the green energy bid. And we just opened a new office in Luxembourg, so I'm a bit stretched right now.'

'I'm extending my coaching practice,' said Saffron. 'When I finish here, I've got an in-depth business transformation session to deliver on Zoom.'

'I've got marking,' growled Mrs Hanratty.

'And as you haven't taken on any other responsibilities…' Heather let the words hang in the air like a bad smell.

Becca raised her hands in surrender. 'All right. I'll take a look at it tomorrow, after school drop-off, and think about it.'

'That's settled, then,' said Saffron. 'Alicia, minute that. Action for Becca. I'll follow up.'

Becca shivered involuntarily.

'Any other business? No? Good.' Saffron stood up and began packing things into her designer bucket bag. 'Heather, can you let me have five minutes? Rosie, I need to touch base with you: playground tomorrow? Mrs Hanratty, we must have a word about accreditation, but we can do that some other time. Thanks, everyone. Oh yes, and the headteacher has assured me he *will* attend the next PTA meeting.' She beckoned Heather over.

Becca took her coat off the back of her chair and put it on. She had expected people to linger for a chat, but they were all striding to the door. *Probably going home to family dinner. Maybe their partners are cooking.* She buttoned her coat and went into the corridor.

Ellie was colouring in a picture, her tongue poking out with concentration and one of her mousy plaits working its way free of its bobble. 'Here's your mummy!' said the teaching assistant brightly. 'She's been good as gold,' she added, standing up, gathering the coloured pencils and dropping them in the pot. 'Come on, Ellie, time to go home.'

Becca helped her daughter on with her coat and located the mitten which, as always, was halfway up her left sleeve. 'What's for dinner, Mummy?'

'Spaghetti bolognese,' said Becca.

'Ooh, yummy,' said the teaching assistant.

'Hopefully,' said Becca, though she didn't hold out much hope for the jar of sauce and the own-brand pasta sitting on the kitchen counter. She took Ellie's hand and followed everyone else into the playground.

'You took *ages*, Mummy,' said Ellie, pulling on her hand. 'What were you doing?'

Becca considered how to answer. Making friends . . . no. 'Helping with school stuff,' she said, eventually.

'Ooh. Like what?' Their footsteps sounded unnaturally loud in the darkness. Becca hurried Ellie along until they were on the well-lit street.

'Um, I'm really not sure.'

2

Becca kissed Ellie on the cheek. 'Go on, trouble, you'd better get in line. The bell will ring any minute.' *And if you're in the line, maybe one of the other kids will talk to you.* She was worried that after two weeks at school, Ellie would chatter happily to her about Mrs Shaw, her class teacher, and Mrs Daniels, the teaching assistant, but hardly ever mentioned a classmate. *Make friends, Ellie. Don't be like me.*

'Mrs Shaw won't come out for ages,' said Ellie, bottom lip protruding, blue eyes round and sad. 'We're always last.'

'You should still be in line, ready for her.' Becca eyed the old-fashioned bell on the wall, waiting for someone to tug it into noisy life.

'OK, Mummy,' said Ellie, and skipped off to the line. Just as she joined it, the bell rang. Ellie looked round and waved at her. 'Bye, Mummy!'

'Bye, Ellie, have a good day!' Becca called. She edged backwards to the wire fence. She couldn't leave, not until Ellie was safely in school, but she could prepare for a quick getaway.

Or she could have done if it wasn't for Mrs Shaw. The lines of bigger children – not much bigger, but still –progressed jerkily into the school, with occasional deserters running back for a forgotten lunchbox or dropped mitten, but the reception class fidgeted on the playground like new recruits waiting for the arrival of the sergeant major.

Just when Becca thought they would be there all day, the reception class door opened and Mrs Shaw walked outside. 'Good morning, everyone!'

'Good morning, Mrs Shaw,' the line chorused raggedly.

'We've got lots to do today, so let's come inside quickly and quietly.'

Cheek, thought Becca. *You're the one who's kept us standing here.*

The children filed in immediately, only occasionally knocking into the child in front, dropping something, or turning to wave to their parents yet again. Finally the last child made their way through the door, which was abruptly pulled shut.

Becca let out a relieved breath and scuttled to the gate, but the other parents had beaten her to it. There was already a queue to leave, complicated further by two women, both towing wailing children, trying to get into the playground. Becca leaned against the fence and waited. *At least that's not me*, she thought. *Just imagine.* Today was the latest she had dared to leave it, arriving in the playground five minutes before the bell was due to ring. She was pretty sure Saffron and Heather would be in the junior playground, if they weren't cutting deals over croissants and coffee, but best not to take any chances.

The queue was dwindling now, and she joined it. Ten minutes at a fast walk and she would be at the flat, putting the kettle on and searching a job site or two. Maybe.

'*There* you are.'

Becca's heart sank. Saffron, of course, resplendent in her furry gilet and a matching fur hat which looked as if it ought to belong to the Queen of Narnia. *Don't accept any Turkish Delight.* While Saffron was smiling, her tone conveyed that Becca ought to have been quicker about getting to a place where she could be apprehended.

'Hi, Saffron,' Becca ventured.

'I'm sure you're on your way to the book swap,' said Saffron. 'Unless you've already visited?'

'Well, I—'

'What am I saying? Of course you haven't. I checked it when I was bringing my two in and it's still a disgrace. But now that you've taken it on…'

'Yes,' said Becca, faintly.

'I knew we could count on you,' said Saffron, patting her on the shoulder. 'I've just been chatting with Declan – the headteacher, you know – and I assured him you would restore the book swap to its former glory.'

'Thank you so much,' said Becca.

'My pleasure,' said Saffron, and gave her a smile more suited for a child who had managed to put the round shape in the round hole of the shape-sorter. 'Oh Rosie, do you have that five minutes you promised me?' And she was off, her knee-high leather boots squeaking as she hastened to apprehend another hapless parent.

Becca sighed. *Stitched up like a holey sock.* She ambled to the gate – presumably even Saffron wouldn't tell her to hurry – and followed the wire fence in the opposite direction to the way she would normally go. Towards the book swap.

***

The closer Becca got to the red phone box on Beech Lane, the more fervently she hoped for a miracle. Not that she was religious, but if some divine being had pulled a blinder out of their box of tricks…

However, it was not to be. With every step the windows of the book swap grew grimier and the books within more untidy. In the front window was a sheet of lined paper with *BOOK SWAP* written on it in wavering capitals. At least, that was what Becca presumed it said. One side had come unstuck and the sign had swivelled round, so in reality it said *OK AP*.

Maybe it'll be better when I open the door. Maybe the books themselves are fine. Maybe it just needs Blu-Tack, a damp cloth and a bit of a tidy. She gripped the tarnished silver handle and pulled. Then she let go and stepped back, her nose wrinkling of its own accord. 'Oof.'

What was that smell? Becca sucked in a lungful of fresh air and considered. It combined the mustiness of old books with bottom notes of wet dog and perhaps an accent of urine. She moved cautiously forward and peered through the glass. The books sat higgledy-piggledy on the shelves, in some places two deep, while elsewhere there were gaps like missing teeth. Horror novels loomed over mysteries, while steamy-looking romances snuggled up to children's books.

Becca felt in her pocket and found a clean tissue to cover her nose and mouth. She steeled herself, then advanced and wrenched the door open again.

The smell persisted even through the handkerchief. Becca glanced at the floor, half expecting to see a puddle, but presumably it had dried. *What if there are mice? Or rats?* She let go of the door and walked away, hearing it creak then clunk shut. *Like a coffin lid in a horror film, or the front door of a haunted house.*

11

She wiped her fingers on the tissue and wished she still carried hand sanitiser. *There's no way I'm dealing with that*, she thought, her mouth setting in a firm line as she marched down the street. *If Saffron wants it doing so badly, she can do it herself. I'll tell her I'm jobhunting – no, I am jobhunting. I'll start as soon as I get home. Anything to make sure I never have to open that door and smell that smell ever again.*

3

Becca hurried through the drizzle to school. It had been a trying day. She had, as she had promised herself, begun looking for jobs. This had involved searching the website of the local newspaper on her phone, then the various job boards. 'If I had a car...' she muttered. 'Or I didn't have to work within school hours, or the buses weren't rubbish.'

She pinched the bridge of her nose and scrolled through the list yet again. There was one – School Administrator, part-time, not Ellie's school, but one a short bus ride away. But... She eyed the list of duties. *It's been so long...*

She had always intended to go back to work after maternity leave, but Phil had convinced her it was a bad idea. 'Childcare costs are ridiculous,' he had said. 'You'd end up paying to go to work. It would actually save money if you stayed at home. You could take

Ellie to playgroups and things.'

'I suppose… But I like my job and the team are great. I don't want to give up work.'

'It wouldn't be for ever. Just while Ellie's little, until she goes to school… Maybe when the preschool grant kicks in you could find something part-time. Or get an Avon round, if you can't find a proper job. You could wheel Ellie round with you.'

She was lying on the sofa, exhausted, with Ellie fast asleep in the crook of her elbow, having dropped off in the middle of a feed. 'Becca,' Phil said, and she turned her head on the cushion, too tired and too apprehensive about waking Ellie to move any further. 'Face facts. I work away a lot. How will you cope with holding down a job and looking after a baby?'

And that was that. Becca had stayed at home, working through never-ending piles of washing and ironing, cooking meals to tempt Ellie, who was a fussy eater, then making dinner for when Phil got in, usually late. In return, just before Ellie's third birthday, Phil met Ariane on one of his work trips. She was twenty-four, dynamic, didn't have milk stains on her top, and kept up with current affairs. 'She takes care of herself,' he had said, in explanation. 'Works out, gets her nails done, that sort of thing.'

'I'd work out and get my nails done if I had any spare time or money,' said Becca.

'No you wouldn't,' said Phil. 'When you put Ellie

down for the night you stare at the TV like a zombie.'

Becca opened her mouth to defend herself, then closed it. Things dragged on uneasily for a few more months, mostly because Becca was too overwhelmed by the idea of starting again with nothing in the bank. Phil had weaselled his way out of marrying her when she became pregnant. *Always an excuse*, she thought, as she wiped the dining table following another messy meal. *Let's have a proper wedding once the baby's born, Becca... We can't afford a wedding and a baby, Becca... There doesn't seem much point now, Becca... What a fool I was.*

Eventually, though, after several heavy hints, Phil had offered her money to help with the rent until she found her feet, and Becca had moved into a small flat half a mile away. Her parents had urged her to move back home with them in Scotland – they had never taken to Phil – but pride kept Becca from complying. She had thought staying near what she knew would help, but gradually people drifted away. Or perhaps she'd pushed them away. She wasn't sure which.

She looked at the advert again. 'Who would employ me?' she asked herself. 'They probably wouldn't even give me an interview.' She swiped out of her browser, put the phone face down, and went to make herself a cup of tea. A hot drink would warm her up, and there would be no need to put the heating on.

She had kept herself busy by giving the flat a good clean, then going to the cheapest food shop in the village to pick up some bits and pieces. There was a cheaper supermarket in town, but that would involve taking a bus, an expensive bus, and carrying it all home. Something was bound to go wrong. She had checked the shop windows and the village noticeboard for job opportunities, too, but there had been nothing.

As she trudged along the road which led to the school, wrapped up in a big coat, scarf, gloves and woolly hat, Becca remembered Froggy, her little green runabout, who had run like a dream until the day he wouldn't start and was pronounced not worth fixing.

'We don't really need two cars,' Phil had said. 'Everything you need is a short walk away. We could go down to one car and save money. And it's good for the environment. We'd still have mine for the big shop.'

'Good for the environment,' she muttered, as the cold wind found its way between the loops of her scarf and stung her neck. Cars glided past, parking as close as they could to the school, and parents got out, exclaiming at the weather.

As usual on wet days, it took even longer for the classroom doors to open. Becca waited, shifting from foot to foot, hands rammed in her pockets, but by a small miracle, the reception-class door opened first. Mrs Daniels stood there, looking for the parent to match each child. Becca craned her neck, but she didn't see Ellie.

Child after child was reunited with their parent, but still Becca waited. At last, when the strands of hair that had escaped from her hat were thoroughly damp, Ellie appeared. Becca waved and Ellie made to go to her, but Mrs Daniels held her back, scanning the playground in every direction but Becca's.

She stepped forward. 'I'm here.'

'Oh yes, so you are,' said Mrs Daniels. 'Silly me. I didn't recognise you, all wrapped up.'

'It's raining,' said Becca.

'Yes, well. See you tomorrow, Ellie. Don't forget to tell your mummy what you've got in your bag.' She released Ellie, who ran to Becca and took her hand.

'What have you got in your bag?' Becca asked, as Ellie towed her to the gate. 'Let me put your hood up.'

'Books!'

'A new reading book? We haven't finished the last one.'

'No, for the book swap! A big girl brought them. I have to give them to you. Because you run the book swap.' Something in Becca's face changed Ellie's excitement into confusion. 'That's right, isn't it, Mummy? Mrs Shaw said you did. And she said I was a sort of book monitor.' Ellie puffed her chest out.

'She said I should have a badge.'

'Did she,' said Becca.

'Can we go now?'

Becca opened her mouth to say that it was raining and they'd do it tomorrow, then changed her mind. *If Ellie sees it, dirty, smelly and damp, she'll understand why I don't want to look after it.* 'Yes,' she said, and they turned away from home.

Becca's footsteps slowed as they approached the phone box, even grimmer through a filter of rain, but Ellie pulled her towards it. 'Come on, Mummy! Let's put the books in.'

Becca opened the door. 'Just put them on the shelf, Ellie, anywhere will do.'

Ellie slotted the books carefully into one of the gaps. There were three: a phonics book, a picture book about The Elves and the Shoemaker, and something called *Beast Quest*. 'There,' she said, with satisfaction. 'I'll tell Mrs Shaw, then everyone will know. Maybe they'll bring books too.'

'Maybe,' said Becca. 'Let's head home before this gets worse.'

Ellie skipped by her side, her mittened hand in Becca's. 'We went to the book swap!' she sang. 'We went to the book swap!'

Becca looked down at her. 'Did you like it?'

'Yes,' said Ellie. 'But it's sad.'

'It's dirty,' said Becca. 'The books aren't in any

18

order. And it smells.'

'That's why it's sad,' said Ellie. 'We can make it feel better, can't we?' She gazed up at Becca. 'Can't we?'

There was no way out. 'Yes.'

'Hooray!' Ellie did an extra big skip. 'I'll make a new sign at home. We can tidy it after school tomorrow.'

'Maybe,' said Becca. She pulled out her phone and checked the weather forecast for the next day. Sunny. But Ellie wasn't setting foot in that phone box until it was less disgusting, which meant she would be cleaning it while Ellie was in school tomorrow.

'I'll use my best felt tips,' said Ellie. 'The ones Daddy gave me. And I'll put the sign in my bag to show Mrs Shaw tomorrow.'

'Yes, why not,' said Becca. And as she wondered what she had got herself into, a gust of rain hit her in the face.

4

'Are you going to the book swap today, Mummy?'

'Yes, Ellie, to clean it. Now please will you put your shoes on? We'll be late if you don't hurry.'

'I'm excited.' Ellie sat on the little stool by the front door of the flat, her toes in one shoe, gazing up at Becca. 'Can we go after school? So I can put my sign up?'

'Yes, but only if you get your shoes and coat on in the next two minutes.'

Ellie rammed her feet into her shoes, then stood on tiptoe to unhook her coat. She couldn't quite manage it and Becca unhooked it for her, laughing. 'Maybe the book swap isn't such a bad thing if it gets you to stop daydreaming!'

'Is daydreaming bad?' asked Ellie. She put her left arm in the sleeve and tried to pull the coat round herself.

'No,' said Becca, 'not at all. Just inconvenient sometimes, when people are in a hurry.'

'Is the book swap bad?'

Becca sighed. 'No, just messy.' She secured Ellie's flailing right arm and guided it into her coat sleeve.

'I nearly did it, Mummy,' said Ellie.

'I know. We'd better get moving.'

Ellie didn't move. 'You forgot something.'

Becca patted her pockets. Purse, phone, keys waiting on the hook. 'I don't think so.'

'Cleaning stuff? For the book swap?'

'I'm going to the book swap later, Ellie. I'm not lugging a load of cleaning products to school with me. Now do come *on*.' Her tone was sharper than she had intended, and Ellie's lip quivered.

'Are you cross? I'm sorry, Mummy.'

'It's OK.' Becca gave her daughter a gentle hug, then got her keys. 'Come on, time to go.'

They arrived in the playground as the reception-class line was filing in. Becca kissed Ellie on the top of her head and half ran with her to the line. Of course, Mrs Shaw was at the head of it. 'Good morning, Ellie,' she said. 'Did you get held up?'

'We were having a discussion,' said Becca.

'Ahh,' said Mrs Shaw, and looked very wise. 'I'm sure we'll see you bright and early this afternoon.'

Becca thought about saluting, but decided the potential consequences for Ellie weren't worth it.

21

'Sure,' she said, and watched Ellie file into the classroom.

Back at the flat, she checked the cupboard under the sink for materials. There was a half-pack of J-cloths, rubber gloves, some all-purpose cleaner, and a duster with holes in it. *I don't mind throwing that away.* She found a tote bag, and as an afterthought put in a can of Febreze she had bought when Phil dropped his kebab in their sitting room after a late-night session. The smell had lingered for weeks. Finally, she boiled the kettle, quarter-filled a bucket with hot soapy water, then stuck a mop in it. *This is probably overkill,* she thought, eyeing the small pile sitting by her front door.

The book swap looked marginally less dingy today. Becca assumed that was the effect of the sunshine rather than any actual improvement. She set down her bucket gratefully, pulled on the gloves, and opened the door.

'Oh, for heaven's sake.' A carrier bag sat on the floor, books spilling out. She picked up a couple. One had no cover, and a couple of loose pages fluttered to the ground like dead leaves. Becca bit back a swearword, seized the bag and dumped it on the pavement. She reached for the Febreze and sprayed it liberally in the air. Finally, she put on a fabric mask she had found stuffed in a drawer and set to work.

The floor of the book swap responded surprisingly

well to being mopped. After a couple of goes, the dirt began to lift. Becca smiled as she pushed her mop into the corners. 'That's better, isn't it?'

You're talking to a phone box.

Becca's face grew warm. Perhaps that was the exercise, though. *So what?* she thought. *No one's around to hear me.* She inspected the water in the bucket, which looked as if an alligator might raise its head any minute. 'That'll do,' she said, and put the bucket outside. 'Now for the windows.' She took down the *OK AP* notice and rummaged in her bag of supplies.

But no matter how much all-purpose cleaner she squirted on the glass, most of the grime refused to shift. Becca wondered whether the windows were tinted until a small clear patch appeared and made the rest of the glass seem even dirtier. *It's ridiculous*, she thought, throwing down her cloth in disgust. *At this rate I'll need a whole bottle of this stuff for one bit of glass.* Then she glanced at the shelves. Her eyes gleamed above her mask and she reached for a duster.

A few minutes later the duster was scored with dark lines, but the shelves were noticeably cleaner. Becca took off her mask and inhaled slowly. The book swap was still a bit musty, but not actively unpleasant. Her eyes watered, but that was probably disturbed dust. *Historic dust. And that's mostly gone.* She inspected the duster. *Hot water will fix that.*

'Right, that's enough for now,' she said. 'I'll come back when I know what to do about the windows.' She reversed out of the phone box, turned and—

'Oof!' She collided with a white open-necked shirt.

'Oh, sorry,' said the man wearing it. He was in his late thirties, maybe early forties, pleasant-looking, with dark hair greying at the sides. He was also wearing a smart navy suit, which made the orange plastic bag he was holding seem incongruous. 'I was just—' He held up the bag.

Becca's eyes narrowed. 'Are you dumping those?'

'Not dumping, exactly.'

Becca held out a hand for the bag, and on receipt, peered in. Children's books, well past their best days. She extracted one at random and stared at its ripped cover. 'Do you think this is fit to go into the book swap? Really?'

'OK, maybe not that one, but I'm in a bit of a rush, so—'

'So you're dumping them here for me to deal with,' Becca snapped. 'Thanks a bunch.'

He sighed. 'Look, I'm on my way back from a meeting. The charity bookshop was closed.'

'Whatever. Off you go. You carry on being busy and important, and I'll deal with this.'

He stepped back, raising his hands in surrender, and Becca was gratified to see a mark on his shirt.

'Won't happen again, if that makes you feel better.'

'It's a start,' said Becca, and watched him walk to his car. He got in and buckled up, and it glided away without a sound. *Electric. That figures.* She turned to the book swap. 'If any of those books are worth keeping, I'll let Ellie put them in later.' She emptied her bucket into a nearby drain, packed up, and set off home.

As she walked, she found herself speculating about the book dumper. *Unusual to see a man in a suit dropping off children's books. Wonder what he does? Maybe he's a single parent like me.*

Or maybe his wife knew he was passing the charity bookshop and handed them to him when he was leaving this morning. 'Can you do something with these? The kids have grown out of them, and it's only five minutes out of your way.' Becca wrinkled her nose, then stopped at the front door of the flats, put the bucket down and fished in her pocket for keys.

Once home, Becca put everything away and washed her hands. She studied herself in the bathroom mirror: hair scragged back in a ponytail, her face framed by a couple of sweaty strands. She had a smudge of dirt on her forehead, and the mask had left faint red lines across her nose and cheeks. She giggled. *I'm not surprised you scared him off!*

She treated herself to a quick shower, then settled on the sofa to go through the bags of books.

25

Occasionally the book dumper came to mind, but when he did, she shoved him out again and carried on.

5

'I was hoping I'd catch you.'

Becca turned, guilt sending a shiver down her spine, though she wasn't sure what to be guilty about. There was bound to be something.

Standing beside her was a woman who seemed vaguely familiar. 'Rosie,' she said. 'We met at the PTA.'

'Oh. Yes. Sorry, I—'

'I wanted to say that you're doing a great job with the book swap. I passed it on my way here and it's looking much better. Those windows were a disgrace before. And it doesn't smell!'

Becca felt her face flush for what seemed to be the tenth time that day. 'Oh, it wasn't anything, just Febreze and vinegar and a good scrub.' *The cheapest vinegar I could find*, she added, to herself. She had been amazed at how it cut through the greyish-brown film that coated the glass. *If it doesn't still smell like a chip shop, Ellie can put up her sign.*

'I'll get Eva and George to go through their bookshelves and pass on anything they've outgrown,' Rosie said. 'I wouldn't have put them in the swap before, because it was so smelly and dirty that it would have ruined them.'

'I suppose,' said Becca. *It's a vicious circle*, she thought. *People put their tatty unloved books there, so no one goes, the book swap gets worse, and the books get worse.* 'Thank you,' she said. 'I'll check the shelves and remove anything that shouldn't be there.'

'That's a good idea,' said Rosie. 'Do you need any help? I mean, we're all busy, but—'

'No, it's fine,' said Becca. 'I can manage.'

'Mummy!'

It was Ellie's voice. She was at the reception-class door, practically jumping up and down with frustration.

'Sorry,' she said. She held out her hand and Ellie ran to her.

'I thought you'd never look, Mummy,' she scolded. 'Can we go to the book swap now?'

Becca rolled her eyes, mostly for Rosie's benefit. 'I feel as if I've spent all day in the book swap. But yes.'

'Let me know when there's room for more books,' said Rosie, and drifted towards the door for year two.

'I've got more books,' said Ellie. 'And the sign.

Mrs Shaw said it was lovely. She put a marble in the jar. That's my first marble.'

'What does that mean?'

Ellie gave a little sigh. 'When the jar's full, we get a class treat.' She gazed up at Becca. 'Didn't you have marbles at school?'

***

Ellie skipped as they neared the book swap. 'It's clean!'

'It's certainly cleaner,' said Becca. 'Hopefully it'll stay that way.' The leaves on the tree by the phone box had begun to turn. The afternoon light caught them, transforming each into a bright gold coin.

'Mrs Shaw gave me this for the sign.' Ellie rummaged in her school bag and produced a folded blue paper towel, in which was a ball of Blu-Tack.

'Oh good,' said Becca. 'I didn't think of that.'

'Mrs Shaw did,' said Ellie, with an air that suggested Mrs Shaw was a superior human being.

'Good for her. Let's put your sign up. Ooh, wait – let's take a picture of you with it first.'

Ellie stood in front of the book swap, held the sign up and beamed. One of her socks was falling down. Regardless, Becca snapped a picture on her phone. Then she divided the Blu-Tack into four, pressed a piece into each corner of the sign and opened the door of the book swap.

'Careful, Mummy! Don't break the glass.'

'Don't worry.' Becca made sure the sign was straight and pushed it into place.

'Can I look?'

'Yes, but don't go in the road.'

Ellie ran a few steps, then turned. Joy spread over her face. 'Everyone will know it's a book swap now!' She ran back, pulled four books from her bag and handed them to Becca, one by one.

When she came to the last book, she didn't let go. 'Mummy…'

'Yes, Ellie?'

'Could we borrow this? It looks fun.'

Becca glanced at the cover. *The Magic Key*, it said.

'I like Biff and Chip,' said Ellie, 'but I haven't read this one yet. I'm on Pink band. This is Blue band.'

'Then we'll borrow it,' said Becca. 'We can put it in the book swap when we finish it, or maybe you could put in a book you don't read any more.'

Not that Ellie had many books. Phil had objected to book-buying on the grounds that there was a perfectly good library nearby and she would only grow out of them. But the perfectly good library was where they had lived before. Phil gave her an allowance for Ellie, which he said was more than he was obliged to do. However, once the bills were paid and food bought, plus school uniform and essentials, little was left for luxuries such as books. Books were Christmas and birthday presents or occasional surprises from Gran and Grandad, not a way of life.

Ellie put the book in her bag. 'Can we read it tonight? I won't know all the words, but I'll try.'

'I know you will, sweetheart,' said Becca, and hugged her.

***

The next day, once she had dropped Ellie at school, Becca nipped home to collect the things she had left ready. She returned to the book swap with several bags for life, cleaning materials, and a set of collapsible steps. It was sunny again, and she had to admit the phone box was looking much brighter, not just because of the pink and blue flowers on Ellie's sign.

'Right,' she said. 'A bit of outside work, then sorting the books.' She placed the steps, climbed up, and wiped the dirt from the front *TELEPHONE* sign. 'That's better: people can see you properly now.' She leaned back to admire her handiwork and nearly overbalanced at a loud honk behind her.

Becca grabbed the top of the steps to steady herself, glared at the passing car, then giggled. *Someone said hello.* She turned to the book swap, gave it a little pat, and climbed down. She moved round the box until all four signs were clean.

She opened the door and gazed at the shelves, then began checking through them. Once you'd taken out the really shabby books – and there weren't many –

the rest was fine. It just needed organising.

She grouped books in categories: thrillers, mysteries, non-fiction, romance, and children's books on the bottom shelves where they could be reached. As she searched through the shelves, she frowned. *Those weren't there before.* Three books that belonged together. She pulled one out. *His Dark Materials: Northern Lights*, she read. It wasn't new – it had definitely been read – but it was in good condition.

Someone must have dropped them off, she thought, and felt a little glow inside. For the first time in longer than she could remember, she was proud of herself. 'See, people are bringing you nice things,' she said to the book swap. She smiled, and carried on sorting the books.

6

Gradually, word spread. Ellie's school bag contained a book or two for the swap every day, often with a little note saying thank you. When the book or two became five, six or seven, Becca asked Mrs Shaw whether it would be possible to have a book-swap box somewhere in school that she could collect from.

'What a good idea,' said Mrs Shaw. 'That might be a library project.'

A week later, she summoned Becca in the playground. 'The library helpers have found and decorated a box and it will live in reception,' she said. 'If you're calling into the office, you can take a look.'

'Thanks,' said Becca. She could feel her cheeks and her neck going pink.

Once Ellie had gone into the classroom, Becca went round to the main entrance and rang for admission, rather overawed. She half-expected to be told off but someone buzzed her in. And in the foyer was a large cardboard box, covered in red and blue stripy paper and decorated with stuck-on multicoloured letters: *BOOK SWAP BOX*. There was already a small pile of books inside.

'Are you the book-swap lady?' asked the receptionist. Her badge said *Angie*. 'I've got a sign for you.' She reached below the counter and produced a large piece of card. On a cream background was a collage: two rows of bunting. Each flag had a letter on it, spelling out *TAKE A BOOK, LEAVE A BOOK*.

'Oh!' said Becca. 'It's lovely. Who made it?'

'The library helpers,' said Angie. 'They're very active.'

'Wow. Can you say thank you to them for me?'

'I'll let the English lead know. Will you take the books, too?'

'Oh yes, I should, shouldn't I?' Becca bent over the box to hide her embarrassment. 'Shall I call in once a week?'

'That seems sensible.'

Becca made a hasty exit, sign and books tucked under her arm.

The sign would just fit above the top shelf of the book swap. Becca wondered if one of the enterprising library helpers had visited and measured up. She tried to remember what she had done in the last years of primary school. Nothing so useful, certainly.

She slipped the books from school into a convenient gap among the children's books and stepped back, sign in hand.

'What are you doing?'

Becca jumped. Standing nearby was a middle-aged woman in jeans and a puffer jacket. Her hair was in a tight ponytail, erupting in a mass of blonde curls at the top of her head.

'I was just— I take care of the book swap. I need to fetch some steps to put this sign up.' She displayed the sign and smiled, but her smile faded beneath the woman's unblinking gaze. 'Um, do you like books? It's free. You can take one if you want.'

'I'd like the time to read,' the woman said, stony-faced. 'I'd like the time to mess around playing house with a phone box.'

'I'm sorry, I—'

'I do the early clean at the school, you see, and now I'm off to my next job.'

'I am looking for a job,' said Becca, humbly.

'Are you really,' said the woman, and snorted.

'Well, not at this exact moment, but I've just dropped my daughter at school.'

'You don't have to make excuses to me,' said the woman. 'You carry on with your book box.'

'Um, thanks,' said Becca, but the woman was already walking away. Her trainers squeaked on the pavement.

Becca walked home, watching out for the woman, skirting any bus shelter where she might be waiting. She carried the sign facing inwards, suddenly ashamed to be seen with it. *I shouldn't be doing this. I should be applying for jobs or starting a business. I should be doing something to improve Ellie's life. And mine. Learning skills, if nothing else. Not messing about with this.*

But they asked me to do it.

And you always do as you're told, don't you?

She winced, and quickened her pace.

Her phone buzzed as she pulled out her keys. *I'll look when I get in*, she thought, manoeuvring the sign carefully through the doorway.

When she checked her phone, she was glad that she had waited.

Hey Bex, I can't take Ellie this weekend. Something's come up. Next weekend should be fine though. I'll send you a bit of money to buy her a treat, so she knows I'm thinking of her. Make sure you say it's from me. Phil

Becca sighed, imagining Ellie's disappointed face. She still believed in her father and Becca did her best not to interfere with that, even when Phil was at his most annoying. Even when he called her Bex, which she hated. She flicked the kettle on and hit *Reply*.

Thanks for letting me know. Make sure you do take Ellie next weekend, she loves spending time with you.

Becca

To be entirely honest, she wasn't sure that Ellie did love spending time with her father. When asked, Ellie always said she had had a nice time and showed Becca a trinket or a new hair bobble, but she never seemed enthusiastic. Phil ought to spend time with her, though, as her parent. Weekends had been agreed, and even if he managed two-thirds of them, maybe less, it was better than nothing.

Becca made herself a cup of tea and eyed the sign, propped up in the tiny hallway. *It can't stay here. Besides, the library helpers will expect to see it. And Ellie probably knows about it too.* She sighed, took a gulp of her tea, which was still far too hot, and went in search of something to put the sign up with.

***

Becca moved cautiously, burdened with steps, the sign, and a bag containing sticky tape, Blu-Tack and scissors. Then she realised the woman who had accosted her earlier would be at work by now, and relaxed.

'Back again,' she said as she reached the book swap, and looked around before patting it on one corner. She opened the door, balanced the sign on a shelf, and unfolded her steps.

As she had thought, the sign fitted snugly above the top of the shelves. It wouldn't need much to hold it. She found the Blu-Tack and pressed the sign in place. 'There.' She nodded at the sign and descended the steps.

As she did, something caught her eye. A book spine: *Wyrd Sisters – Terry Pratchett*. It was at her eye level. She had read a couple of Terry Pratchett books, but not this one. She reached for it, then paused. *It looks—* She took the book out to confirm it. *It looks new.* The spine was uncreased, the cover pristine. *Could it be the same person as before? The one who left the His Dark Materials books?*

She felt guilty for taking the book, as if she was stealing it. *I'll put it back when I've read it*, she reasoned. *It's meant to be borrowed. It's a book swap.* Nevertheless, she hid the book in her bag, and was glad to be on her way home.

She meant to read just a few pages, to see what the book was like. She only noticed the time when her stomach growled. *Oh dear.* She put a couple of slices of bread in the toaster. *I'll eat a quick lunch and check the job sites.* But somehow the book found its way into her hand again, and then she was too far through it to stop. *If I finish it, I can get on with what I should be doing.*

She read the last page, sighed a long, satisfied sigh and checked her phone. She had ten minutes until she needed to set off for school pickup. On impulse, she went to the chest of drawers. In the top drawer was a pad of letter paper and a few matching envelopes, possibly a relic of a school penpal long ago.

Becca found a pen and pondered what to say.

Thank you for leaving Wyrd Sisters at the book swap, she wrote. *It was very kind, especially as the book looks new. If you don't mind, I'll keep it for a little while to reread. I read it so quickly that I might have missed bits.*

Can I ask whether you also left the His Dark Materials books?

Thank you again,

Becca

PS I'm looking after the book swap temporarily.

She addressed the envelope – *To the person who left a copy of Wyrd Sisters here* – put the note in and stuck down the flap. Then she grabbed her coat, put the envelope in her pocket, and hurried to collect Ellie.

7

Two days later, at pick-up time, Ellie was at the classroom door when it opened. 'There's Mummy!' she cried, and Mrs Daniels let her go with a smile. 'Guess where we went today!' She barrelled into Becca, knocking the breath out of her, and wrapped her arms around her hips.

'I have no idea,' said Becca, laughing, when she got her breath back. 'Where did you go today?'

'We went to the book swap! It was a class trip for two of our school values.'

'Your which?' Ellie was quite muffled, and Becca wondered if she had heard right.

'Our *values*, Mummy. We had to put bright-yellow jackets on and walk in pairs. Olivia asked me to walk with her.'

'Oh good. Is Olivia your friend?'

'Of course she is, Mummy,' said Ellie, with a note

of exasperation in her voice. 'Anyway. Mrs Shaw was at the front and Mrs Daniels was at the back. We all took a book from the big box and put it in the book swap. Mrs Shaw says we have to visit with a grown-up and choose a book.' Ellie finally came up for air. 'Can we go now?'

'Could we make it next week?'

Ellie's jaw dropped. 'Mummy!'

Becca laughed. 'It was a joke. Come on, then.'

She said goodbye to Claire and Debs, two other reception-class mums she had started chatting to on the playground. Ellie gripped her hand, as if worried she might go the wrong way, and they set off.

If anything, Becca felt guilty. She hadn't returned to the book swap since leaving that note. Partly because she wasn't sure she wanted to know whether there was a reply, or even that it had been picked up, but also because she had spent too much time there recently. Instead she had cleaned the flat, tackling everything from light fittings to skirting boards. She had also overhauled her wardrobe, removing the tops and leggings faded and stretched out of shape through years of wear. She put them in a charity bag, and when she tied the handles together and left it by the gate she felt several pounds lighter.

'So what are the school values?' she asked.

'One is responsibility, for keeping the book swap tidy. Mrs Shaw says you have the main responsibility.

41

And when she said "Ellie's mummy" everyone looked at me!'

'Gosh,' said Becca. 'I suppose I do. What was the other value?'

'Community, because the book swap is part of our village and it's for everyone. There are three other values, too. Come on, Mummy, I'll race you!' Ellie ran to the phone box and pulled at the door, but couldn't open it. 'Mummyyy!' she wailed, then burst out laughing.

She isn't the same child, thought Becca as she hurried over. For a moment she felt a pang that Ellie didn't need to cling to her any more, then shook it off. *Once she would never have dreamt of running ahead and she'd have waited for me to open the door. Now she wants to do things herself.*

That's probably school, she thought, as she opened the door for Ellie, who immediately began searching for her book. *But this helps, too.* And she ran her hand along the bright-red paintwork.

'Here it is,' said Ellie, pulling out *The Highway Rat*. 'This is the book I put in.'

'Oh yes,' said Becca. 'That's nice.' She glanced at the shelves automatically to check their neatness, and froze.

Propped against the books on a higher shelf, well past a child's reach, was a white envelope with *Becca* written on it in neat black pen.

Becca took it down and stood looking at it.

'What is it, Mummy?' Ellie asked. 'Is it for you?'

'It has my name on it,' said Becca.

'Then it's for you. Aren't you going to open it?'

'Maybe later,' said Becca, and shoved it in her jeans pocket. 'Now, are you taking that book home, or do you want to choose another?'

Ellie spent ten minutes flicking through different books and putting them back neatly before deciding that yes, she would take *The Highway Rat*.

***

At the flat, Becca settled Ellie at the kitchen table with a colouring book while she made her toast.

'Mrs Shaw?' said Ellie.

Becca paused, butter knife in the air. 'I think you mean Mummy.'

'Sorry, Mummy,' said Ellie. 'Can I go to the toilet, please?'

'Of course you can,' said Becca. 'You don't have to ask.'

'We do at school,' said Ellie. She slid off her chair and ran out.

Becca chuckled, then fished the envelope from her pocket and ripped it open.

Dear Becca,

Thank you for your note, and I'm glad you enjoyed the book. Of course you can keep it to reread, if you like.

I wanted to thank you for looking after the book swap. It needed someone to take it in hand, and it is much better now.

Thank you for stepping up, from all of us.

Becca stared at the letter until she heard the toilet flush. Quickly, she stuffed the letter in the envelope and rammed it in her pocket. She wasn't sure what she had expected, but she felt . . . disappointed. *Why didn't the person sign it? They obviously don't want me to know who they are, for some reason. And who's 'all of us'?* She unscrewed the lid of the jam as if she was wringing its neck and stabbed the knife into it.

8

Walking to school with Ellie the next morning, Becca felt eyes on her. *What have I done now?* But her conscience was clear. *You're imagining it. Why would anyone be looking at you?*

They entered the playground and immediately, Rosie came over. 'I'm so sorry,' she said, putting a hand on Becca's arm.

'Have I missed something?' Becca asked.

'I don't think Becca knows, Rosie,' said Claire.

Becca frowned. 'What don't I know?'

'We're really sorry,' said Claire. 'It looks bad, but I'm sure it'll clean up.'

'What will?' Rosie bit her lip. *What could it possibly be?* 'Just tell me!'

'The book swap,' said Rosie, and Becca's heart sank. 'It's been vandalised, but it isn't too bad. I mean, they haven't set fire to it or anything.'

Ellie's grip on her hand tightened. 'What's vandalised, Mummy?'

'Don't worry, Ellie. Some silly people have messed about with the book swap, that's all.'

'*Our* book swap? Why?' Ellie gazed up at her, her eyes suspiciously shiny.

'Don't cry, Ellie. They're just silly people who don't know any better.' The bell rang, early for once, and Becca wondered if one of the staff had spotted her. 'Please don't worry, sweetheart. I'll go there now and see what needs doing.'

'The person who did it,' said Ellie, and Becca had never seen her so cross. '*They* don't know our values.' And she flounced off to the line.

***

Becca was one of the last to leave the playground that morning. Rosie and Claire had asked if she would like them to come too, but she had refused on the grounds that she was a big girl. She considered going home and making a strong cup of tea to help her face it, but she knew that if she did, she wouldn't go back. So she gritted her teeth and marched down the road.

The book swap was still standing, but the bright red was streaked with black aerosol paint. As Becca drew nearer, she saw a few windows had been smashed. Books were in a heap on the floor, some with their covers ripped off. The sign the library helpers had made lay in four jagged pieces.

'I'm so sorry,' Becca whispered. She could barely speak for the lump in her throat. She put her hand on a corner that hadn't been graffitied. *I took care of the book swap, and for what? For someone to come along and ruin it. What's the point of caring if this is what happens?*

She rubbed the paintwork slowly, then realised what she was doing and stopped. *It's just an old phone box. It can't feel. You're projecting your own feelings onto it.* Even as she thought it, anger rose in her. *Why shouldn't I? Everyone left me alone when Phil and I split up, and I turned into a mess. No – I was already a mess, thanks to Phil. If it hadn't been for Ellie…* She put her other hand on the phone box, not caring about paint or dirt. *That's why the book swap is so important to me. I know what it's like to be abandoned.*

A leaf fluttered down and landed at Becca's feet. She blinked, hard.

'Excuse me?'

Becca almost jumped out of her skin.

The speaker was a woman, perhaps in her sixties, wearing black trousers and a red blazer and holding a clipboard. Next to her stood a man about the same age in a grey suit.

'Excuse me?' the woman repeated. 'Is this a good time?'

'Does it look like a good time?' Becca replied, and

47

clamped her mouth shut to keep in a sob.

'Well, not really, but I take it this is the community book swap?'

Becca swallowed. 'It was until somebody vandalised it. It was absolutely fine yesterday, and now look at it.'

'You're obviously upset,' said the man.

'Yes, I am,' said Becca. 'If I find out who did it, I'll wring their neck. No, better than that.' She turned to the book swap and took a picture with her phone. 'I'll report this to the police. I'm not having it.'

'I completely understand,' said the woman. 'Would you mind answering a few questions?'

'Yes, I would. I've got a crime to report. And once the police are finished, assuming they come at all, I've got to clean this up and put everything in order.' She opened the photos app on her phone, scrolled until she found the photo she had taken of Ellie, grinning in front of the book swap, and thrust it under the woman's nose. 'There. That's what it's supposed to look like.'

'I see,' said the woman.

'Anyway, what do you want?' asked Becca. 'Are you doing a survey?'

'In a way,' said the woman. 'But we've taken up enough of your time. Thank you very much.' And she strolled off with the man.

Becca watched them go, passing a short, stout

woman on crutches, and forced herself to face the book swap again. The panes would need replacing – not to mention clearing up the broken glass – and lots of books would have to be thrown away. Maybe the library helpers wouldn't even make another sign, after what had happened.

'This is a mess and no mistake.' The woman leaned on her crutches and gazed up at the book swap. 'Who let it get like this? I hand it over for a few weeks while I get my hip sorted, and this happens.'

'It was fine until today,' said Becca. 'Someone's done this overnight.' Then the penny dropped. 'You must be Mrs—'

'Mrs Walentynowicz,' said the woman. 'Most people call me Mrs Val. I prefer that to having my name mangled. Anyway, what did you tell those two?'

'I didn't exactly tell them to mind their own business,' said Becca, 'but I might have implied it.'

'Oh dear,' said Mrs Val, grinning. 'I bet they didn't like that.'

Becca shrugged. 'Does it matter?'

'It does if you want Meadley to win Best-Kept Village. I've seen that pair round here before. They're the judges.' And as Becca stared at her in horror, Mrs Val broke into a wheezy laugh.

9

Becca hurried home, head down, cheeks burning. *Of all the times to speak your mind... When people find out, they'll probably never speak to me again. I'll be thrown out of the PTA. Hopefully Ellie won't be bullied...*

You told them the truth. And you're stressed. People will understand.

They don't usually.

'You're not thinking straight,' Phil would have said. 'You're getting emotional. Hormones.' At that point she had usually gone into another room. Otherwise she would have shouted at him in front of Ellie.

She quickened her pace until she was almost running.

Back at the flat, she made herself that strong cup of tea and looked up the police non-emergency number.

'I wish to report a crime,' she said, when the call was answered.

'Right,' said the man on the other end of the line, sounding rather impressed. 'What sort of crime?'

'Vandalism. Someone's graffitied the book swap in Meadley and smashed its windows.'

'The . . . book swap?'

'Yes. It's an old phone box near the primary school, on Beech Lane.'

A pause. 'So it's not your property.'

'No, it belongs to the community. I was hoping someone could come and – and take fingerprints?'

'Mmm. So no one was seen doing it?'

'Not as far as I know,' said Becca. 'It happened overnight.'

'Very unlikely to be CCTV down there, and not much chance of fingerprints, to be honest with you.'

'So you won't do anything?'

The man sighed. 'Of course we'd like to get an officer to the scene of every crime, however minor. It's resources, you see. What I will do is inform your local community support officer: he'll call in when he's next in the village. Can I take your name and number, please.'

Becca gave them, so quietly that the call handler had to ask again, then sat brooding.

It is a minor crime, in the scheme of things.

Yes, but it's stupid and pointless. Whoever did it

should be brought to justice.

They won't be. She closed her eyes and saw the book swap, graffitied and broken. She tried to remember it as it had been, bright, clean, and filled with interesting books, but the image was blurred as if it had never been real at all.

Will I ever be able to restore it to what it was? What if the vandals return?

You won't know unless you try. Besides, you'd better clear away that broken glass before someone cuts themselves.

Becca imagined a small child reaching towards a broken pane and immediately jumped out of her chair.

***

She was sweeping up the last of the broken glass when an irregular tapping made her look round.

'Only me,' said Mrs Val. 'Not that I can do much, but I thought you might like company. I live down the road and saw you passing. And I'm supposed to do short walks with these things. Well, my daughter said I wasn't allowed to leave the house without her. But she also said that if I did I was to use crutches.'

'Oh. Thanks.' Becca gave the floor of the book swap a final sweep, then emptied the dustpan carefully into a bag she had brought for the purpose.

'I can take that if you want,' said Mrs Val. 'Put it in my recycling bin.' Balancing carefully, she slipped the handle of the bag over the grip of her crutch.

A car stopped and the driver wound down his window. Bruce Springsteen at full volume almost blew Becca's hair back. 'What's happened?'

'Vandalism,' said Becca. 'I reported it to the police but it's low priority for them, so I'm cleaning it.'

'Got a few panes out,' said the man.

Becca sighed. 'Yes. Luckily they haven't left any jagged edges. I've just cleared up the glass.'

'My brother's a glazier, lives in Meadhurst but works here too. I'll drop him a text, see if he'll come by and look at it.' The man picked up his phone, took a picture, and typed a few words. They heard a whoosh. 'There. Well, hope you get it sorted. I'd lend a hand, but I've got to be somewhere at ten o'clock. I'll try and come down later.'

'Thank you,' said Becca, barely able to believe it. What luck that someone with the power to help them had happened to drive by. She stared after the diminishing car, misty-eyed.

'*Are* you going to clean it?' asked Mrs Val.

Becca rolled her eyes. 'That's the plan, yes.'

'What are you using?'

'I'll try vinegar, and if that doesn't work I'll have a think.' She poured vinegar on a soft cloth and began to rub the paintwork.

A few minutes later, the black paint was faded but still visible.

'Gonna be a long job,' said Mrs Val, who was

leaning on her crutches, watching. 'I reckon you need something stronger.'

'I do too,' said Becca, 'but I don't want to damage the paint. The book swap's been traumatised enough already.'

Another car pulled up and Claire got out. 'Hi Becca, how's it going?'

'Slowly,' said Becca, indicating the faded patch of spray paint.

'I might be able to help,' said Claire. 'My husband works in chemicals – solvents and things, don't know what exactly – so I asked him what would get spray paint off a phone box. He said this would probably do it.' She reached into the side bucket of her car door and held up a brightly-coloured spray bottle. 'I checked online, not that I don't trust him but just to be sure, and the internet agrees. Maybe test it on a hidden bit first.'

Becca read the back of the bottle. *Use in a well-ventilated area.* 'We're outside, anyway.' She shrugged, sprayed a tiny bit on a fresh cloth, then went to the side of the book swap furthest from the road and gave it a tentative rub. She half-expected a genie to appear.

The cloth came away filthy, revealing glossy red paint.

'Wow!' Becca had another go to make sure it wasn't a fluke. 'Thanks, Claire! You've saved me a day of scrubbing.'

'No problem,' said Claire. 'What will you do with those books?' She waved a hand at the small heap of torn, battered volumes sitting on the pavement.

'No idea,' said Becca, as she cleaned. 'I guess they'll have to be recycled.'

'One of the school mums makes book sculptures,' said Claire. 'You know, those folded thingies you sometimes see – apples and hearts and hedgehogs – made out of old books. I bet she'd take them. Maybe she'd make one for the book swap.'

'Really?' Becca considered what sort of sculpture would suit the book swap. And as she thought, another car stopped behind Claire's.

10

A man in a white shirt and suit trousers got out of the car and approached them. 'I'm Tim Jameson, from the *Meadborough and District Times*. Is one of you...' He took a phone from his pocket and consulted it. 'Becca?'

What on earth does someone from the local paper want with me? Claire nudged Becca and she raised a timid hand to shoulder level. 'That's me.'

'Oh good. I saw a post on social media about the book swap being vandalised and I decided to come and see for myself.' He inspected the phone box. 'You're doing a grand job fixing it up. It looked shocking in the photos.'

'Thank you,' said Becca. 'I've had lots of help, though. Claire brought cleaning stuff, and Mrs—' She turned to Mrs Val. 'I'm terribly sorry, could you tell the reporter your name?'

'Mrs Walentynowicz. I can spell it if you like.' She leaned on her crutch and extended a hand to the reporter, who shook it gently. 'I'm in charge of waste disposal.' She tapped the carrier bag. 'We have a glazier stopping by later.'

'Excellent,' said Tim. 'Do you mind if I take notes? And could I get a quote or two?'

'Yes, of course,' said Claire, and Becca's heart beat a little faster. *I'm going to be in the local paper.* She wasn't sure if she was more excited or apprehensive. She also wasn't sure what she thought about the possibility of Phil reading whatever they wrote. No doubt he would think her activities a waste of time. But did his opinion matter?

'Great,' said Tim. 'People should understand the importance of community assets like this. I'm planning to phone the headteacher at the primary for a quote, too.'

Claire looked past him. 'You won't need to do that, Tim. Here he comes now.'

Becca followed her gaze with interest. She hadn't actually met the headteacher of Ellie's school yet. When she had visited the school, on a tour for prospective parents booked at the last minute, the deputy head had shown them round—

She gasped. Walking towards them, in what looked like the navy suit he had worn on that fateful day, was the man who had tried to dump a bag of books at the book swap. The man who had practically run away from her. And she had made it pretty clear what she thought of him. *Oh, heck.*

'Hello, Mr Cole,' said Claire.

'Hi,' he said, smiling. 'Hello, Tim. And hello, Mrs Walentynowicz. Good to see you back.'

Becca hoped her face wasn't as red as she suspected. She glanced down at herself. Her jeans were grubby and she was wearing the final shapeless old top she had kept for cleaning, accessorised with yellow rubber gloves.

'You must be Becca,' he said. 'I'm Declan Cole, the headteacher at Meadley Primary. You're Ellie's mum, aren't you? In Mrs Shaw's class.' He offered a hand.

Becca took off her glove, wiped her hand on her jeans, and shook it. 'That's me,' she said. 'I didn't realise you were— I'm sorry I was a bit abrupt. You know, when—'

He laughed. 'I deserved it. I should have done a quality check on those books.' He turned to Tim. 'Becca does a fine job of looking after the book swap.'

Becca brushed a sweaty strand of hair off her forehead and wished the ground would swallow her up. 'Anyone could do it,' she muttered. 'And I haven't been doing it that long, anyway. Only while Mrs...' She took a deep breath and went for it. 'While Mrs

Walentynowicz was out of action.'

'I'm not sure *anyone* could take care of the book swap,' said Declan Cole. 'Even if that were true, most people don't. We need more people to take on jobs like this. Indeed, some of our pupils visited the book swap this week as part of our commitment to the school values.'

'Responsibility and community,' said Becca. 'Ellie told me.'

'There you are,' said Declan. 'This is important to the whole school, from reception onwards. Once the book swap's back to its normal self, we'll have a grand reopening. Bring the children down, cut a ribbon, get someone to do a speech…'

'Ooh yes,' said Claire. 'Maybe people could walk to school afterwards and have refreshments. Any excuse to eat cupcakes.' She grinned.

'Sounds like a plan,' said Declan. 'I daresay the paper could send a photographer.'

'For a load of cute schoolkids and a feel-good story?' said Tim. 'Absolutely.'

'You should get a photo of these three for the paper now, though,' said Declan. 'Their efforts ought to be recognised.'

'Oh no,' said Becca, before she could stop herself. 'I bet I'm a right state.'

Claire grinned at her. 'You look fine, Becca. Glowing with health.'

So I am a red sweaty mess. She pushed her hair back and sighed, then grew even warmer as she saw Declan Cole looking at her.

Tim checked his watch. 'I have an appointment in the village, so shall I return in a couple of hours? That'll give you time to freshen up.'

Becca could have hugged him. 'I'll carry on here for a bit first,' she said. 'Get the book swap ready for its close-up.' *But what a shower I'll have when I've finished.*

Mrs Walentynowicz chuckled. 'Fame at last,' she said, and swung her way slowly down the lane, the carrier bag on her crutch spinning.

'I should get back to school,' said Declan. 'Tim, if you need anything, drop me an email. Oh, and Becca…'

'Yes?' Becca paused, cloth in hand, wondering what a busy headteacher in a smart suit could possibly have to say to her.

He smiled at her. 'I'm glad you enjoyed the book.'

11

Becca strolled through the school gate and pressed the doorbell. 'I'm here for the PTA,' she said to the intercom.

'That's Becca, isn't it?' said Angie. 'Come on in.' Becca heard a buzz and pulled the door. As she walked down the corridor, she looked at the wall displays. More than one included a red phone box.

The room was perhaps half full when she arrived. 'Hi, Becca,' said Rosie, as Becca unwound her scarf. 'Ooh, is that a new top?'

Becca smiled. 'It is. Ellie said I should buy myself a treat from my first pay packet.'

Saffron came over. 'Oh yes, you're working now. How's it going?'

'Fine, thanks.'

A week or so after the book swap had appeared in the local paper, Becca was apprehended by Angie when she went into reception to collect books. 'I have a letter for you,' said Angie. 'Well, it says *Becca who runs the book swap* on it, which is good enough for me.'

Becca's brow furrowed. 'Who would send me a letter here?'

'Someone who can't reach you any other way,' said Angie. 'Go on, open it. I could use some excitement.'

Becca ripped open the envelope and found a sheet of letterheaded paper.

Dear Becca,

Please excuse me contacting you in this way, but I wasn't sure how else to reach you.

We are looking for someone to manage the Meadborough Hospice charity bookshop in Meadhurst when the current manager retires. None of the volunteers wish to step up, and when we read an article about your work with the book swap in the local newspaper, we wondered if you would be interested.

'Are they having a laugh?' said Becca.

Angie wagged a finger. 'No spoilers, please.'

We have excellent flexible-working policies and the current manager will provide training. If you wish to discuss the role, please call the number above.

Yours sincerely,
Mandy Fairweather
Bookshops Manager, Meadborough Hospice

'Am I seeing what I think I'm seeing?' asked Becca, giving Angie the letter.

Angie skimmed it. 'Looks like it,' she said, with a grin. 'You're being headhunted.'

Becca phoned, then went for an interview, full of nerves and convinced she would be laughed out of the room. When she left, she was still sure she wouldn't last two minutes once they discovered how useless she was. But she had the job, and apparently the administrative skills Phil had dismissed as fit only for dogsbody work would be invaluable.

Claire erupted into the room. 'Late to my first PTA meeting, that's a good start,' she announced, flopping down in a chair. 'I had to bring Josh and he needed a lot of settling. No Ellie, Becca?'

'No, she's sleeping over at her dad's tonight. They're probably watching a princess movie right now.'

Phil had actually phoned her two weeks before. In the evening, too, which was unprecedented. 'Becca, we don't see eye to eye about a lot of things, but I'd like to spend more time with Ellie.'

Becca raised her eyebrows. 'Taking Ellie at weekends when you're supposed to would be a start.'

A long pause. 'I'm sorry. It's hard to fit everything in, I guess. But I want you to know that I'm always there for her.' His voice was slightly thick, and Becca suspected a few beers had brought on an attack of sentimentality.

She got up and closed the door, in case Ellie wasn't asleep. 'What's brought this on?'

'Nothing. Well, um, Ariane says she isn't impressed with me as a parent and I have to do better. Certainly when we have kids together.'

Becca winced, out of habit, then realised Phil's doings didn't matter to her any more unless they affected Ellie.

'Anyway.' Another pause. 'Anyway, I'll definitely have Ellie this weekend, and for a sleepover in the week too. If that's convenient.'

Becca wondered whether Ariane was in the room, holding up cue cards. 'Ellie has an after-school club on Wednesdays and she's going to tea with a friend on Friday, but her other weeknights are free. I'll have to talk it over with Ellie first, though.'

Her first weeknight alone had felt strange, as if a vital part of her had gone missing. But she had cooked herself prawn risotto (Ellie wouldn't touch prawns), watched a romcom, and enjoyed herself tremendously.

The door opened again and Declan Cole hurried in. 'Sorry I'm late . . . got held up on a phone call.' He sat down and put his phone on silent mode.

Saffron cleared her throat and everyone looked her way. 'That's quite all right, Declan. Let's get started. Our main business, of course, is the Christmas fair. Our major players are in position, obviously, but there's the matter of the games…'

Becca volunteered to run the tombola, while Rosie plumped for hook-a-duck and Claire for the coconut shy. 'If I'm dealing with kids throwing things, I'd better stick to the non-alcoholic mulled wine,' she said ruefully.

'*You* can,' said Mrs Hanratty. 'Those of us involved in the carol concert may well indulge.'

The remaining stalls were settled, a winning design chosen for the cover of the carol-concert programme, and progress reports given on the technology update and the year six French exchange. 'Any other business?' asked Saffron.

'I have,' said Becca. 'The school's adoption of the book swap is featured as a case study on the Best-Kept Village website, and also on several platforms encouraging young readers.'

'Was that from your press release?' asked Saffron.

'I believe so,' replied Becca. 'Thanks for sending me a template. It helped a lot.'

'Any time,' said Saffron, inclining her head graciously.

'I take it everything is running smoothly, now that

you've gone part-time at the book swap?' said Declan.

'Yes, it is. The volunteer rota is working really well and the book swap social-media feeds are getting lots of views. Mrs Walentynowicz is posting at least once a day on Twitter, Facebook, and Instagram, and she's shared the password with the volunteer team for us to post too.'

Declan laughed. 'She never ceases to surprise me.'

Saffron leaned forward. 'Anything else to add, anyone? No? In that case, let's wrap up. I need to be on with Chicago in twenty minutes.'

Everyone got up and began putting on coats. 'Want a lift, Becca?' asked Claire.

'I'm fine, thanks,' Becca replied. 'It's a nice night for a walk. It's such a change to go anywhere without a little hand pulling me forward or back.'

Claire grimaced. 'Tell me about it.'

As people dispersed, Becca wrote a couple of reminders in her pocket notebook, then stood up and reached for her coat. Declan was still sitting at the table, typing on his phone. Everyone else had left.

'I thought that went well,' said Becca.

He looked up. 'Yes, it did. Lots of progress.' He put his phone down. 'Um…'

'Could I ask you a question?'

His eyebrows knitted slightly. 'Er, yes?'

'That note you left me, at the book swap. Why didn't you sign it?'

He fiddled with his phone. Then he met her eyes, and to her surprise his cheeks were slightly pink. 'I suppose… It's a bit silly.'

'Go on. I won't laugh.'

'Well, as I was writing the note, in haste as usual, it started sounding more and more official. Really headteachery, and I didn't want to come across that way. I have enough of that here, at school.'

Becca smiled. 'I imagine you do.' She paused, studying him. 'So why did you admit it was you? You didn't have to.'

'Because it felt dishonest. I mean, who leaves anonymous notes? And besides, I like meeting people who enjoy the same sort of books as I do. What's the point of hiding?'

'Exactly,' said Becca. *That's what I was doing. Hiding in my flat, scared to engage with anything or anyone in case I got hurt again. And it took a battered old phone box to drag me out of it.* 'What's your favourite Terry Pratchett book?' she asked, to lighten the mood.

'Not sure. I tend to prefer the Sam Vimes ones.'

'My favourite characters so far are Tiffany Aching and Nanny Ogg,' said Becca.

'I'm not surprised. We should have a proper book chat sometime.'

Becca half-expected him to get up from his chair, to say that he had a report to write or policies to review, or whatever headteachers did, but he didn't. He stayed sitting there, looking at her. 'Ellie's at a sleepover tonight,' she said. 'So if you wanted to, I don't know, go for a coffee somewhere and talk books…'

'My kids are at their mum's during the week,' said Declan. 'There's a country pub on the road to Meadhurst that does good coffee, if you're OK with that? I can drop you off afterwards.'

'Sure,' said Becca. She could barely hear herself over the thudding of her racing heart.

In no time at all they were in Declan's car, driving silently out of the gates. Declan turned into Beech Lane. 'Those solar lights are doing well,' he said.

Ahead of them, the windows of the book swap glowed with warm light. It stood in a carpet of bright leaves, looking as if it had travelled from another place.

As they passed, Becca saw the neat rows of books waiting to be read. With the hand furthest from Declan, she gave the book swap a little wave, and watched it in the wing mirror until it was a bright dot in the distance.

What To Read Next

The Book Swap is a slightly sideways move for me, as I usually write mysteries! However, if you've enjoyed this book, I have suggestions…

If you like contemporary books with books in them (so to speak), you might enjoy my *Magical Bookshop* series. This six-book series combines mystery, magic, cats and of course books, and is set in modern London.

When Jemma James takes a job at Burns Books, the second-worst secondhand bookshop in London, she finds her ambition to turn it around thwarted at every step. Raphael, the owner, is more interested in his newspaper than sales. Folio the bookshop cat has it in for Jemma, and the shop itself appears to have a mind of its own. Or is it more than that?

The first in the series, *Every Trick in the Book*, is here: http://mybook.to/bookshop1.

If you love modern cozy mysteries set in rural England, *Pippa Parker Mysteries* is another six-book series set in and around the village of Much Gadding.

In the first book, *Murder at the Playgroup*, Pippa is a reluctant newcomer to the village. When she meets the locals, she's absolutely sure. There's just one problem: she's eight months pregnant.

The village is turned upside down when a pillar of the community is found dead at Gadding Goslings playgroup. No one could have murdered her except the people who were there. Everyone's a suspect, including Pippa...

With a baby due any minute, and hampered by her toddler son, can Pippa unmask the murderer?

Find *Murder at the Playgroup* here: http://mybook.to/playgroup.

And if you fancy a modern cozy mystery with romance and books included, you might like the *Booker & Fitch Mysteries* series I write with Paula Harmon.

As soon as they meet, it's murder!

When Jade Fitch opens a new-age shop in the picturesque market town of Hazeby-on-Wyvern, she's hoping for a fresh start. Meanwhile, Fi Booker is trying to make a living from her floating bookshop as well as deal with her teenage son.

It's just coincidence that they're the only two people on the boat when local antiques dealer Freddy Stott drops dead. Or is it?

The first book in the series, *Murder for Beginners*, is at https://mybook.to/Beginners.

Bonus Item:

Make your own book hedgehog!

I made one of these a while ago, when one of my kids was poorly and I was looking for something low-pressure that we could do together. They're surprisingly easy to make and they look quite impressive. I made one for the library of the primary school I tutor at, and he's become a library mascot!

There are several free how-to guides on the web, all with a slightly different way of making your book hog. What follows is what I did (and I'm not great at crafts).

You will need:

An old, knackered paperback book you don't want any more. This can be quite short – say 100 pages.

Something to make the eyes, nose and feet. I had a black foam sheet, but you could use card. And if you have any googly eyes, you know what to do.

Scissors and glue (PVA works well).

Method:

Fold the first page in half lengthways, so that the

outer edge of the page is as close to the spine as you can get it. Then fold the top and bottom corners right into the middle, again as close to the spine as you can, so each corner forms a right-angled triangle. This will start to form the body of the hog. Some guides say you have to fold the pages all one way, or change direction part way. I don't think it matters, so I fold all the pages the same way.

Continue folding pages until you have a nice tightly packed semicircle of hog. It will get a bit trickier as the body of the hog grows.

If you haven't already, take off the book covers. Tear off any pages you don't need.

Put one piece of the book cover under your hog and draw round it. Then cut it out, cutting inside the line so that the cardboard won't show on the finished hog.

If you're adding feet, draw some on your foam/card and cut them out. I don't think you need more than two. Put the bit of book cover you've just cut out under your hog, slip the feet into position, and stick the back part of the foot to the book cover. Then stick the book cover onto the bottom of the hog, with the feet between the book cover and the hog.

Cut out and affix eyes and nose in the relevant places.

You can also add ears. I cut out a couple of small teardrop shapes from a spare leaf of the book, then pinched the top of the teardrop in half and stuck each ear between a couple of the folded leaves, above and a little way out from each eye.

And that's it! Behold your book hedgehog! Though you might want to let the glue dry first...

Acknowledgements

My first thanks, as always, are to my brilliant beta readers: Carol Bissett, Ruth Cunliffe, Paula Harmon and Stephen Lenhardt. Thank you for your feedback and suggestions! Any remaining errors are my responsibility.

I was inspired by the book swap in my home village – it has *two* book swaps, but one is much nearer my house! It's a converted phone box like the one in the story, and I'm a regular visitor and swapper. Thank you to those who maintain it, and to everyone who drops off interesting books there.

And of course, many thanks to you, dear reader! I hope you've enjoyed this story, and if you have, please consider leaving a short review or a rating on Amazon and/or Goodreads. Reviews and ratings help books find new readers.

COVER CREDITS

Font: Allura by TypeSETit. License: SIL Open Font License v1.10: http://scripts.sil.org/OFL.
Cover image drawn and coloured by me (please see copyright page).

About Liz Hedgecock

Liz Hedgecock grew up in London, England, did an English degree, and then took forever to start writing. After several years working in the National Health Service, some short stories crept into the world. A few even won prizes. Then the stories started to grow longer…

Now Liz travels between the nineteenth and twenty-first centuries, murdering people. To be fair, she does usually clean up after herself.

Liz's reimaginings of Sherlock Holmes, the Magical Bookshop series, the Pippa Parker cozy mystery series, the Caster & Fleet Victorian mystery series and the Booker & Fitch mysteries (written with Paula Harmon) and the Maisie Frobisher Mysteries are available in ebook and paperback.

Liz lives in Cheshire with her husband and two sons, and when she's not writing or child-wrangling you can usually find her reading, messing about on Twitter, or cooing over stuff in museums and art galleries. That's her story, anyway, and she's sticking to it.

You can also find Liz here:

Website/blog: http://lizhedgecock.wordpress.com
Facebook: http://www.facebook.com/
lizhedgecockwrites
Twitter: http://twitter.com/lizhedgecock
Goodreads: https://www.goodreads.com/lizhedgecock

Books by Liz Hedgecock

To check out any of my books, please visit my Amazon author page at http://author.to/LizH. If you follow me there, you'll be notified whenever I release a new book.

The Magical Bookshop (6 novels)
An eccentric owner, a hostile cat, and a bookshop with a mind of its own. Can Jemma turn around the second-worst secondhand bookshop in London? And can she learn its secrets?

Pippa Parker Mysteries (6 novels)
Meet Pippa Parker: mum, amateur sleuth, and resident of a quaint English village called Much Gadding. And then the murders begin…

Booker & Fitch Mysteries (3 novels, with Paula Harmon)
Jade Fitch hopes for a fresh start when she opens a new-age shop in a picturesque market town. Meanwhile, Fi Booker runs a floating bookshop as well as dealing with her teenage son. And as soon as they meet, it's murder…

Caster & Fleet Mysteries (6 novels, with Paula Harmon)
There's a new detective duo in Victorian London . . . and they're women! Meet Katherine and Connie, two young women who become partners in crime. Solving it, that is!

Mrs Hudson & Sherlock Holmes (3 novels)
Mrs Hudson is Sherlock Holmes's elderly landlady. Or is she? Find out her real story here.

Maisie Frobisher Mysteries (4 novels)
When Maisie Frobisher, a bored young Victorian socialite, goes travelling in search of adventure, she finds more than she could ever have dreamt of. Mystery, intrigue and a touch of romance.

Sherlock & Jack (3 novellas)
Jack has been ducking and diving all her life. But when she meets the great detective Sherlock Holmes they form an unlikely partnership. And Jack discovers that she is more important than she ever realised...

Halloween Sherlock (3 novelettes)
Short dark tales of Sherlock Holmes and Dr Watson, perfect for a grim winter's night.

For children

A Christmas Carrot (with Zoe Harmon)
Perkins the Halloween Cat (with Lucy Shaw)
Rich Girl, Poor Girl (for 9-12 year olds)

WHITE
RHINO
BOOKS

Printed in Great Britain
by Amazon